SALLY

THE SPARROW AND FRIENDS

BY J T SCOTT

SALLY

THE SPARROW AND FRIENDS
BY J T SCOTT

It was a bright spring day in the garden.

Sally the Sparrow needed food for her chicks.

"I will find you something to munch," said Sally.

"If you are good chicks I will bring you some lunch."

When Sally returned from finding food

her chicks had disappeared

and Sally's nest was empty.

"Where are my chicks?"

asked Sally the Sparrow.

"They are only small.

Please help me to find them all."

"While you were out they have all flown away,"

said the Queen Bumblebee.

"Why don't you look around the garden

and find them all today?

There's **Bumper the Bumblebee.**

Maybe he can help you find your chicks?"

"Hello Bumper," said Sally.

"Have **you** seen my chicks?

They have all flown away.

I have to find them all today."

Bumper thought for a moment.

Then he looked up at the sky.

"If your chicks have flown away," he said,

"they may be up high."

Sally looked through her telescope.

"I can't see my chicks," said Sally.

"They're not up high in the sky.

I can see clouds, but no chicks."

"I don't know where your chicks have gone," said Bumper.

"They can't be far away.

Why don't you ask **Boris the Butterfly,**

maybe he has seen your chicks?"

"Hello Boris," said Sally.

"Have **you** seen my chicks?

They have all flown away.

I have to

find them all

today."

Boris thought for a moment.

Then he looked at the red brick wall.

"Maybe your chicks have

flown over the wall," said Boris.

"Shall we have a look?"

Sally looked over the wall.

"I can't see my chicks," said Sally.

"They're not over the wall.

I can see cars and the road

but no chicks at all."

"I don't know where your chicks have gone," said Boris.

"They can't be far away.

Why don't you ask **Chris the Caterpillar,**

maybe he has seen your chicks today?"

"Hello Chris" said Sally.

"Have **you** seen my chicks?

They have all flown away.

I have to find them all today."

"Shall we look under my flowerpot?" asked Chris.

He shuffled to the edge

and tipped

the flowerpot

on to its side.

"I can't see my chicks under the flowerpot," said Sally.

"They won't be there.

It's far too hot."

"I don't know where your chicks have gone," said Chris.

"They are only small.

It should be easy to find them all.

Why don't you ask William and Wendy the Worms?"

"Hello William, hello Wendy," said Sally.

"Have **you** seen my chicks?

William & Wendy's Home

They have all flown away.

I have to find them all today."

"We do hope your chicks

can be found,"

said William.

"But you won't find them here,"

said Wendy.

"They're not underground."

"Why don't you ask **Kirsty the Kitten**,"

said Wendy.

"Maybe she can help."

"Stop causing a fuss,"

said William.

"Go away and don't bother us!"

"Hello Kirsty," said Sally.

"Have **you** seen my chicks?

They have all flown away.

I have to find them all today."

"I haven't eaten them

if that's what you think,"

said Kirsty.

"Maybe your chicks

have gone to the pond

for a drink?"

"I don't think you've eaten them,"

said Sally.

"But where can they be?

I want my chicks to come back to me."

"Why don't you ask **The Three Fish?**"

said Kirsty.

"Perhaps The Three Fish

will grant your wish."

"Hello fish," said Sally.

"Have **you** seen my chicks?

They have all flown away.

I have to find them all today."

"Hello Sally!" said one of the fish.

"We are magic fish.

Ask us anything you want

and we will

grant you a wish!"

"I wish I knew where to find my chicks,"

said Sally.

"They have flown out of the nest,

and got up to some tricks."

"Why don't you ask

Gertrude the Gnome?"

said one of the fish.

"She may know when

your chicks will come home."

"Hello Gertrude," said Sally.

"Have **you** seen my chicks?

Bumper says they're not in the sky.

Boris says they're not over the wall.

Chris says they're not under his flowerpot.

William and Wendy say they are not underground.

Kirsty says she hasn't eaten them.

The Three Fish said to make a wish.

Where can they be?

I want my chicks to come back to me."

Gertrude smiled and reached into her pocket.

"You can end your search Sally my dear.

As you can see,

your chicks are right here."

"While you were out looking for food,

your chicks learned to fly and they were gone for ages.

You looked everywhere to find them

and they were hiding in these pages."

"Thank you everyone for your help today," said Sally.

"I thought my chicks were lost

when they all flew away."

"Now they are tired and having a rest.

All of my chicks have flown back home

and they are asleep in the nest."

SALLY
THE SPARROW AND FRIENDS
BY J T SCOTT

Sally the Sparrow and Friends is dedicated to Mum & D2.

The moral right of J T Scott to be identified as the author
of this work has been asserted in accordance with the
Copyright, Designs and Patents Act 1988.

Copyright © 2020 J T Scott

First published in 2020

ISBN: 9781710645156

J T SCOTT

J T Scott lives in Cornwall surrounded by open countryside,
lots of castles, pens, paper and a vivid imagination.

She has also written the Sammy Rambles series
and created the inclusive game Dragonball Sport.

Sammy Rambles and the Floating Circus

Sammy Rambles and the Land of the Pharaohs

Sammy Rambles and the Angel of 'El Horidore

Sammy Rambles and the Fires of Karmandor

Sammy Rambles and the Knights of the Stone Cross

www.sammyrambles.com

www.dragonball.uk.com

Printed in Poland
by Amazon Fulfillment
Poland Sp. z o.o., Wrocław

60 FACTS ABOUT

QUEEN

VICTORIA I

Published by Sovereign Island UK

Sales and Enquires: sovereignislanduk@gmail.com

Contents

Who is The Queen?

A Queen is a female ruler of an independent state, especially one who inherits the position by right of birth.

1. Victoria was born on 24 May 1819.

2. Queen Victoria I was Queen of the United Kingdom of Great Britain and Ireland from 20 June 1837 until her death in 1901.

The Sovereign's Throne is one of the most important items of furniture in the Palace of Westminster.

Picture of Queen Victoria

Who is The Queen?

3. Victoria was born in Kensington Palace.

4. Victoria was the daughter of Prince Edward, Duke of Kent and Strathearn, and Princess Victoria of Saxe-Coburg-Saalfeld.

Portrait of a young Victoria

There is a statue of Queen Victoria near Kensington Palace. It was sculpted by Victoria's fourth daughter Princess Louise, Duchess of Argyll and erected in 1893.

Who is The Queen?

5. Queen Victoria's birth name was Alexandrina Victoria.

6. Victoria became Queen at the age of 18.

FUN FACT

7. Queen Victoria only started to learn how to speak English at the age of 3. Her first language was actually German.

Who is The Queen?

8. In 1820, both Victoria's father and Grandfather died.

9. Following the deaths of Victoria's father and grandfather, Victoria was raised under close supervision by her mother and John Conroy.

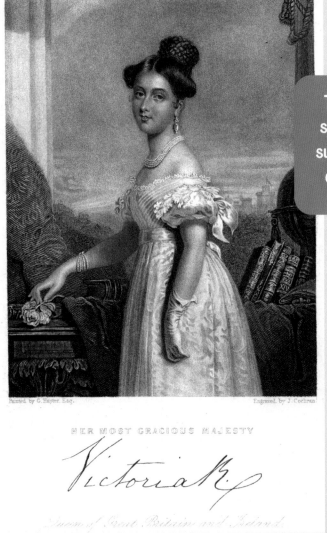

HER MOST GRACIOUS MAJESTY

Victoria R.

Queen of Great Britain and Ireland.

The Line Of Succession is an ordered sequence of named people who would succeed to a particular office upon the death, resignation or removal of the current occupant.

Who is The Queen?

10. Victoria's father was the fourth son of King George III, thus Victoria was not expected to become the Queen.

11. Victoria was known for being very petite, standing at barely 5ft tall.

An Victorian account described Victoria as having "clustered round by glossy fair ringlets"; her complexion "remarkably transparent, with a soft and often heightening tinge of the sweet blush rose upon her cheeks, that imparted a peculiar brilliancy to her clear blue eyes"

Victoria

Who is The Queen?

12. Victoria was an only child.

13. Queen Victoria had the nickname 'Drina'.

While Victoria had no full siblings, she did have a half-sister named Feodora, and they grew up together in Kensington Palace.

Family

Family is a group of persons united by the ties of marriage, blood, or adoption

14. At her time of birth, Victoria was fifth in line to the throne.

15. Victoria's christening took place on 24 June 1819. Victoria was christened by the Archbishop of Canterbury, Charles Manners-Sutton.

The Archbishop of Canterbury is a senior member of the House of Lords, the second chamber of the United Kingdom Parliament. He sits as one of the 26 bishops of the Church of England, who are known as the Lords Spiritual.

Portrait of Queen Victoria

Family

16. In 1830, Victoria became heir presumptive following the death of her uncle George IV.

17. In 1830, The Regency Act 1830 was passed giving provision for Victoria's mother to act as regent in the event that King William IV died while Victoria was still a minor.

All Royals today are direct descendants of Queen Victoria.

Portrait of King George IV

Family

18. Victoria was raised in Kensington Palace.

19. Victoria had a difficult yet very close relationship with her mother who was very protective of her.

Kensington Palace began as a simple Jacobean mansion named Nottingham House, built by Sir George Coppin in 1605 in the village of Kensington.

Picture of Kensington Palace

13

Family

20. Victoria described her childhood as 'melancholy'.

21. Victoria shared bedroom with her mother and was kept away from other children.

Illustration of Old British coin with Queen Victoria

Family

22. Queen Victoria proposed to Prince Albert of Saxe-Coburg and Gotha on 15 October 1839.

23. Queen Victoria and Prince Albert of Saxe-Coburg and Gotha got married on 10th February 1840.

DID YOU KNOW

Victoria and Albert were born just three months apart and were even delivered by the same midwife, Charlotte Heidenreich von Siebold.

Family

24. Initially Albert was not popular with the British public as he was seen to be of a lower class however his popularity grew over time.

25. Queen Victoria fell pregnant within the first two months of her marriage to Albert.

Modern writers have speculated that Queen Victoria may have suffered from postnatal depression after many of her pregnancies as she struggled to bond with her children as newborns and kept her distance from the babies in their early years.

Scenes of Queen Victoria

Family

26. Queen Victoria and Prince Albert had nine children.

27. Prince Albert helped Victoria immensely during her reign. He supported many public causes, such as the educational reform and the abolition of slavery. Albert was also entrusted to run the Queen's household, office, and estates.

It is believed that Prince Albert insisted that all of Queen Victoria's bridesmaids were born "of a mother of spotless character".

Family

28. In 1845, Victoria and Albert bought an estate on the Isle of Wight. Under Albert's supervision, Osborne House was built there.

29. Osborne House was completed in 1851.

Picture of Osborne House

In May 1845, Victoria and Albert purchased the Osborne estate on the Isle of Wight for the sum of £28,000.

In 1848, Albert commissioned Thomas Cubitt to remodel the home.

Family

30. Because of her nine children and 42 grandchildren, Victoria gained the nickname "Grandmother of Europe."

31. Victoria's children were Victoria, Albert "Bertie", Alice, Alfred, Helena, Louise, Arthur, Leopold, and Beatrice.

> Albert played an active role in raising his children (unlike many husbands and fathers in this period).

Picture of Princess Victoria (Queen Victoria's first born)

Picture of Edward VII (Bertie) of England

Family

32. Prince Albert died at 10:50 p.m. on 14 December 1861 from Typhoid Fever.

33. Queen Victoria never recovered from Albert's death and wore black every day for the rest of her life.

A ruling queen's husband is called a Prince Consort because the title of King is only given to a monarch who inherits the throne and can reign.

Prince

Queen

Portrait of Prince Albert

Family

34. Due to Victoria isolation, she was nicknamed 'The Widow of Windsor'.

35. Victoria's youngest son, Leopold, had the disease haemophilia and at least two of her five daughters, Alice and Beatrice, were carriers.

Victoria wanted her sons to grow up like Prince Albert. The only one who resembled his father was Prince Arthur, the third of the boys, later Duke of Connaught. He was Queen Victoria's favourite.

Family

36. Queen Victoria blamed The Prince of Wales philandry, for Albert's early death at 42.

37. After Prince Albert's death, The Queen was hardly seen out in public.

It is widely believed that Edward VII 'Bertie' was Victoria's least favourite child. However, despite her concerns, Edward VII proved to be a popular and capable monarch.

Hobbies and Interests

A hobby is an activity done regularly in one's leisure time for pleasure.

38. Victoria loved to write.

39. Victoria was multilingual.

Queen Victoria kept a journal for most of her life. She wrote her first diary entry in 1832, aged thirteen.

Photo of Queen Victoria with her grandchild

Hobbies and Interests

40. Prior to Victoria's wedding, wedding dresses came in a variety of colours however Queen Victoria opted for a white dress and forbid female attendants from wearing white; this tradition still exists today.

41. Queen Victoria and Albert popularised the custom of having decorated Christmas Trees.

In December 1840, Prince Albert imported several spruce firs from his native Coburg, which kickstarted the Christmas tree tradition in England.

Hobbies and Interests

42. Victoria had a gift for drawing and painting.

43. Queen Victoria frequently went to the opera.

As a young princess, Victoria would draw sketches of her pets, including that of Dash, her favourite King Charles Spaniel.

Hobbies and Interests

44. As a child, Victoria was described as warm-hearted, lively, and occasionally mischievous.

45. Victoria was very fond of singing.

When Victoria was a child her mother used a strict timetable of lessons to make sure Victoria became a clever and good person, as preparation for her becoming Queen one day.

Hobbies and Interests

46. Victoria kept a detailed journal.

47. It is believed that Victoria wrote an average of 2,500 words a day during her adult life.

Queen Victoria's writing style has been described as containing common sense, some simplicity, much shrewdness, and occasional indiscretions.

Palaces and Castles

A castle is a large building, typically of the medieval period and a palace is a large and impressive building forming the official residence of a ruler, pope or archbishop.

48. Shortly after her accession to the throne, Queen Victoria moved into Buckingham Palace.

49. Buckingham Palace was previously owned by Victoria's uncle, King William IV.

Picture of Buckingham Palace

Palaces and Castles

50. Victoria was the first member of the royal family to live at Buckingham Palace.

51. Victoria and Albert spent their honeymoon at Windsor Castle.

Windsor Castle is the oldest and largest inhabited castle in the world and has been the family home of British kings and queens for almost 1,000 years.

Picture of Windsor Castle

Reign

A reign is the time during which a monarch rules.

52. Victoria's reign is known as the Victorian Era.

53. Victoria's reign was marked by a great expansion of the British Empire.

The Victorian Era saw the British Empire grow to become the first global industrial power, producing much of the world's coal, iron, steel and textiles.

Reign

54. The radical expansion of the British Empire meant that many goods entered Britain such as coal, iron, steel and textiles.

55. A great deal of this expansion involved violence and many wars and rebellions took place, such as the Indian Mutiny (1857–59), the Morant Bay Rebellion (1865) in Jamaica, the Opium Wars (1839–42, 1856–60) in China, and the Taranaki War (1860–61) in New Zealand.

Reign

56. At the time when Victoria became Queen, the government was led by the Whig prime minister Lord Melbourne.

57. Victoria was popular at the start of her reign, but her popularity decreased later after she falsely accused a sick lady-in-waiting of an out-of-wedlock pregnancy.

The Victorian Period is often referred to as 'the Golden Period' because it was a time of improvements in society, great achievement, and revolutionary ideas that paved the way for modern times.

Reign

58. During her reign, Queen Victoria survived several assassination attempts including an attempt in 1840, when 18-year-old Edward Oxford fired at the Queen's carriage in London.

59. On 23 September 1896, Victoria became the longest-reigning monarch in history surpassing her grandfather George III.

Portrait of George III

Reign

60. With her impressive reign of 63 years, seven months, and two days, Queen Victoria was the longest-reigning British monarch and the longest-reigning queen regnant in history, until her great-great-granddaughter Elizabeth II surpassed her on 9 September 2015.

The Royal Mausoleum is the final resting place of Queen Victoria and Prince Albert. The Mausoleum is located near Frogmore House, which stands about half a mile south of Windsor Castle in Windsor Home Park.

Glossary

HRH: Stands for "His/Her Royal Highness."

King: The title given to the reigning monarch if that monarch is a man.

Prince: A title given to the husband of a reigning queen, and to the sons and grandsons of the sons of a reigning monarch.

Princess: The title given to the daughters and granddaughters of the sons a reigning monarch.

Queen: The title given to the reigning monarch if that monarch is a woman.

Viscount: The fourth highest ranking in the British peerage.

Words From Author

We hope that this book helped you to learn more about Britain's second longest reigning monarch, Queen Victoria I.

Queen Victoria's reign was a time of great change for the United Kingdom particular due to the massive expansion of the British Empire.

There is still so much to learn about Queen Victoria and so many stories to uncover, we hope that you will carry on learning.

If you enjoyed this book, consider leaving a review and checking out our other books.

Our Titles

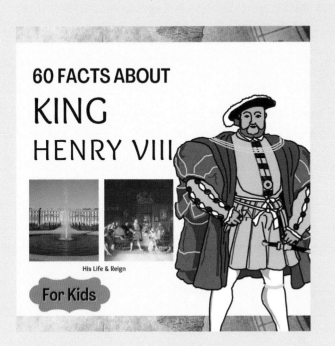

Printed in Great Britain
by Amazon